For Rylan and Kambrie,
with love always
—K.C.

For Junie, who's the dearest
passenger on my Moonlight Train
—A.W.

Text copyright © 2020 by Kristyn Crow • Jacket art and
interior illustrations copyright © 2020 by Annie Won
All rights reserved. Published in the United States by
Doubleday, an imprint of Random House Children's Books,
a division of Penguin Random House LLC, New York.
Doubleday and the colophon are registered trademarks
of Penguin Random House LLC. • Visit us on the Web!
rhcbooks.com • Educators and librarians, for a variety of
teaching tools, visit us at RHTeachersLibrarians.com
Library of Congress Cataloging-in-Publication Data is
available upon request.
ISBN 978-0-525-64543-6 (trade) —
ISBN 978-0-525-64544-3 (lib. bdg.) —
ISBN 978-0-525-64545-0 (ebook)
MANUFACTURED IN CHINA • 10 9 8 7 6 5 4 3 2 1
First Edition • Random House Children's Books supports
the First Amendment and celebrates the right to read.

All Aboard
the
Moonlight
Train

by Kristyn Crow

illustrated by Annie Won

Doubleday Books
for Young Readers

If you're restless and can't sleep,
come explore the jungle deep,
where the beasts and critters creep.
All aboard the Moonlight Train!

There's a toucan at the gate—
takes your ticket, checks the date.
March aboard! Wild things await.
All aboard the Moonlight Train!

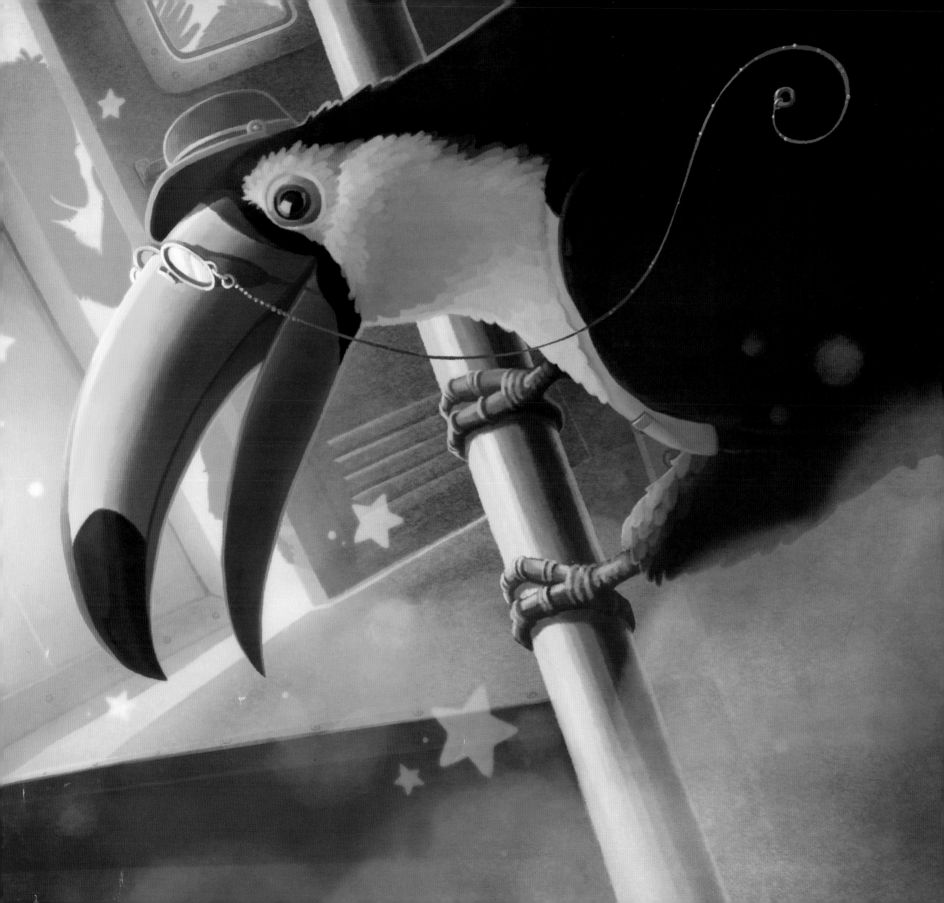

Engine chugging through the trees,
hippos nodding in the breeze.
Spy some hiding chimpanzees.
All aboard the Moonlight Train!

Are the stars out? Go and check.
Climb up a giraffe's long neck.
It's the perfect lookout deck.
All aboard the Moonlight Train!

Winding under sparkling skies,
waterfalls, and fireflies,
watch for bats with glowing eyes.
All aboard the Moonlight Train!

Next, you meet the engineer.
Sound the whistle! Test the gear!
Help make sure the tracks are clear.
All aboard the Moonlight Train!

Hungry for a midnight snack?
Try the mango pancake stack!
Warthogs serve it piggyback.
All aboard the Moonlight Train!

Zebras lead you on a trot
to their favorite sleeping spot.
Dive into a cozy cot.
All aboard the Moonlight Train!

Soon a lion brings a book
from the bedtime story nook.
Snuggle up and take a look.
All aboard the Moonlight Train!

Listen to hyenas croon.
Owls are hooting to the moon.
Rhinos hum a sleepy tune.
All aboard the Moonlight Train!

But before you start to snore—
SHHHHHHHhhhhh . . .
the train stops at your door.
Come back soon! Explore some more!

GOOD NIGHT, GOOD NIGHT,
Moonlight Train!

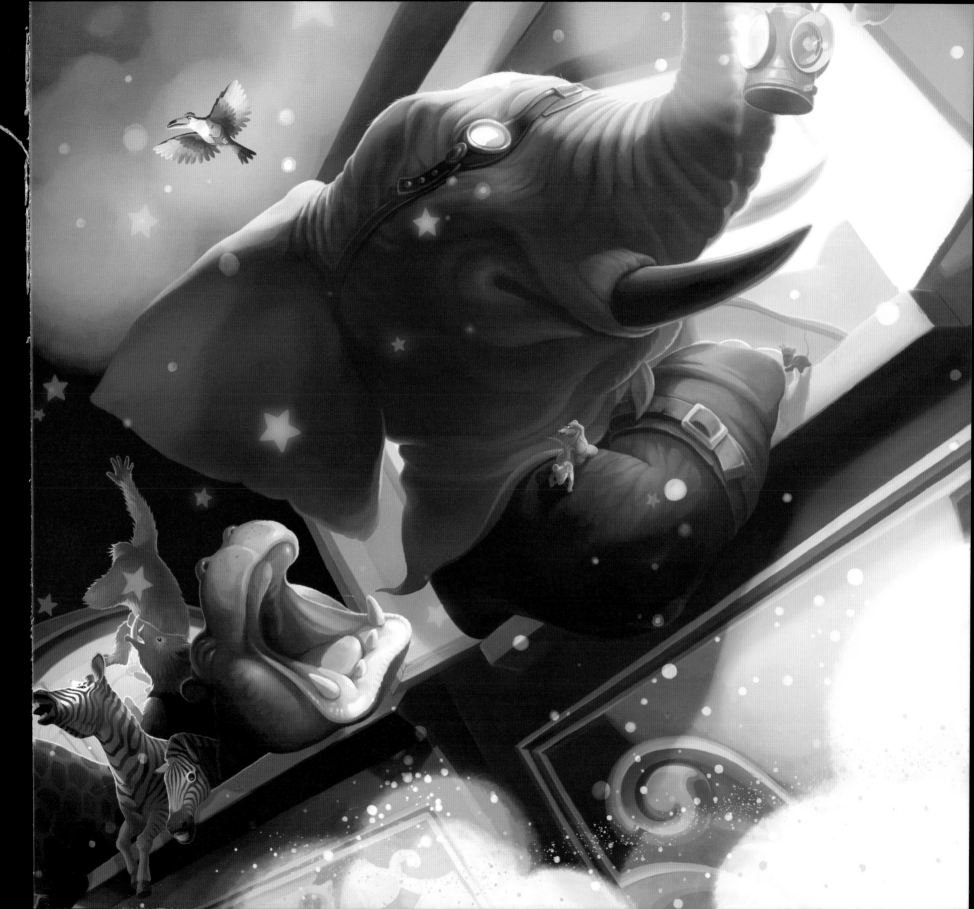